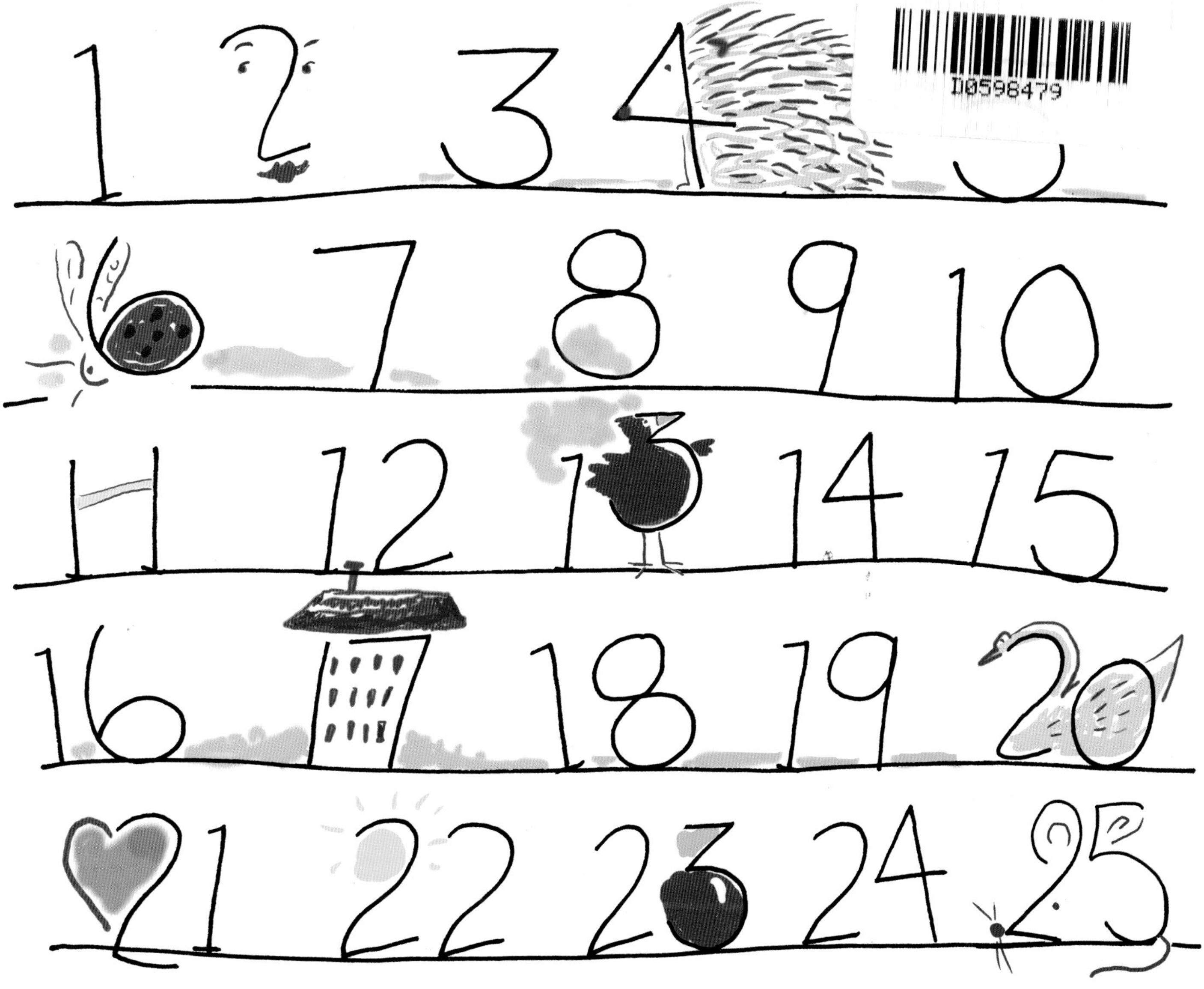
1 2 3 4
7 8 9 10
11 12 14 15
16 17 18 19 20
21 22 23 24 25

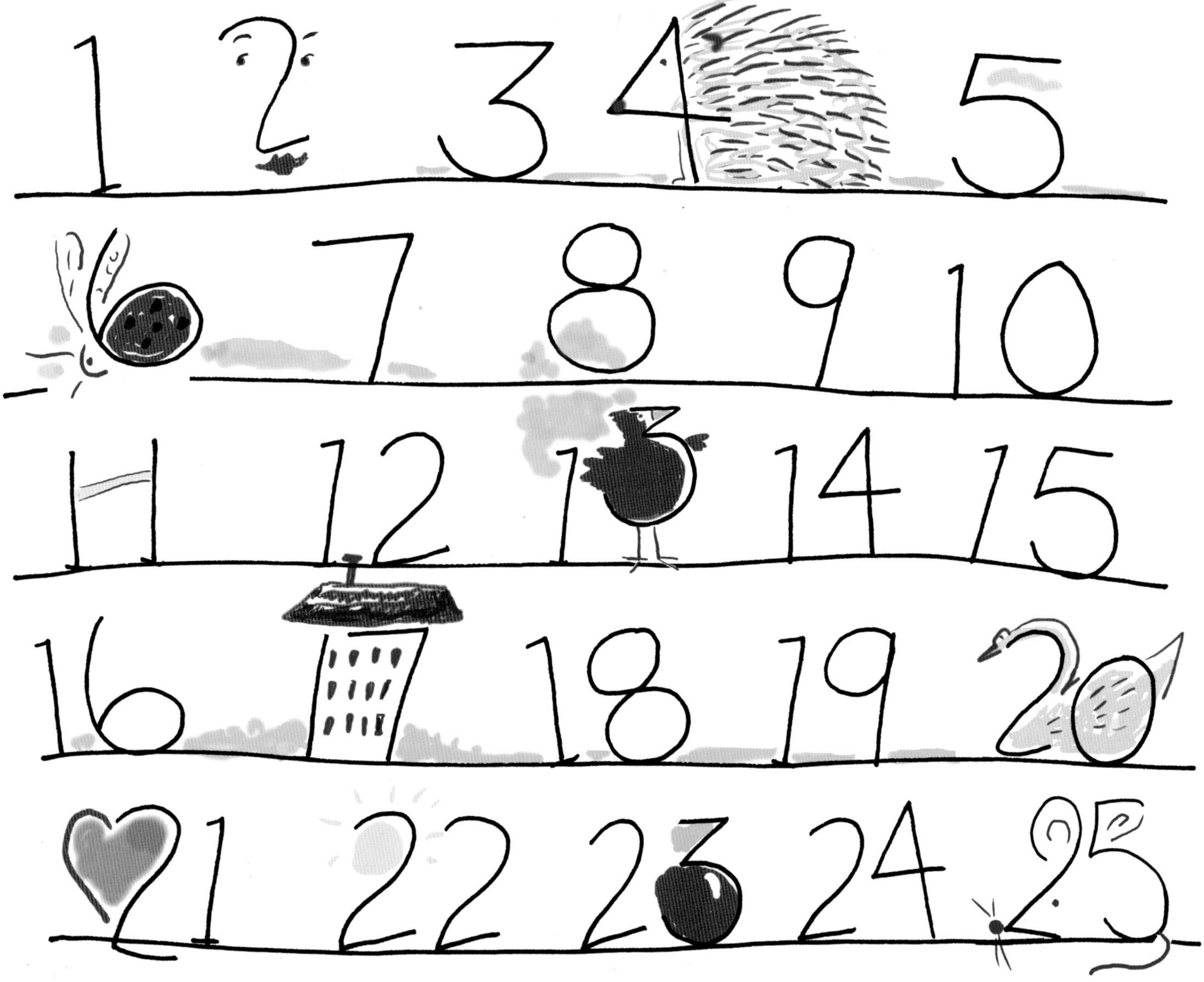
1 2 3 4 5
6 7 8 9 10
11 12 13 14 15
16 17 18 19 20
21 22 23 24 25

2 is for Toucan

Oodles of doodles from 0 to 42

Deborah Zemke

 BLUE APPLE BOOKS

For my daughter, 18.
Thank you for all your help.
—D. Z.

CIP Data is available.
Published in the United States 2005 by
🍎 Blue Apple Books
515 Valley Street, Maplewood, N.J. 07040
www.blueapplebooks.com
Distributed in the U.S. by Chronicle Books

First Edition
Printed in China

ISBN: 1-59354-075-2

1   3   5   7   9   10   8   6   4   2

2 is for Toucan

Numbers are everywhere! From the time your alarm clock wakes you up in the morning, to the number of teeth you brush before you go to bed at night, you are surrounded by numbers. There are even numbers in the water you drink—2 molecules of hydrogen and 1 molecule of oxygen. Numbers tell you about things—how big, how fast, how many. Drawing shows you things, so doodling numbers is like show and tell.

All numbers are made from ten numbers: 0, 1, 2, 3, 4, 5, 6, 7, 8, and 9.

The number 0 is all curves ( ) and 1 is all line. |

The other numbers are made of combinations of curves and lines. 2 5 6 7 8 9

3 and 4 can be written two ways:

3 or 3   4 or 4

Other doodle lines and shapes you'll be using...

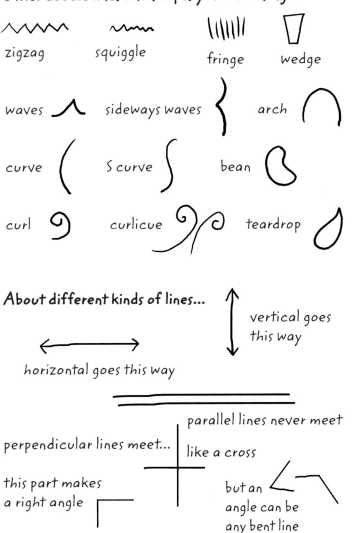

zigzag   squiggle   fringe   wedge

waves   sideways waves   arch

curve   S curve   bean

curl   curlicue   teardrop

About different kinds of lines...

vertical goes this way

horizontal goes this way

perpendicular lines meet...   parallel lines never meet like a cross

this part makes a right angle

but an angle can be any bent line

BASEBALL

What's the count?
Baseball is a game
of numbers:
There're 9 innings,
3 outs, 9 players,
3 strikes, 3 bases,
1 home plate, 4 balls,
batting averages,
earned run averages,
on-base percentages,
runs batted in—
all these numbers
make math our
national pastime!

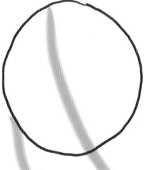

1) Draw an 0.

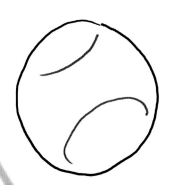

2) Add two curves...

3) and 44 little
red v's.

There are 108
stitches holding
a baseball
together!

4) Now throw
a 90 MPH
fast ball.

You're all nothing
without me!

You're only one without us!

10,000,000,000,000,000,000,000,000,000,000,000,000,000,000,000,000,000,00

Zero may equal nothing, but it makes everything
else worth so much more—like the google you see here.
What's a google? It's the number 1 with one hundred 0's after it.

PARAMECIUM

The paramecium is Number 1! 1 cell, that is. How small is 1 cell? Well, 25,000 of this tiny organism can fit on the head of a pin—though you're more likely to find a paramecium living in a pond, not on a pin.

1) Draw a very tiny 1.

2) Attach a pear-shape blob.

3) Add lots of lines all around.

4) Fill with blobs, dots, and two stars.

Hey! Quit pushing!

We're all you need!

0 1

A computer uses only two numbers, 0 and 1, but it uses billions of them at a time!

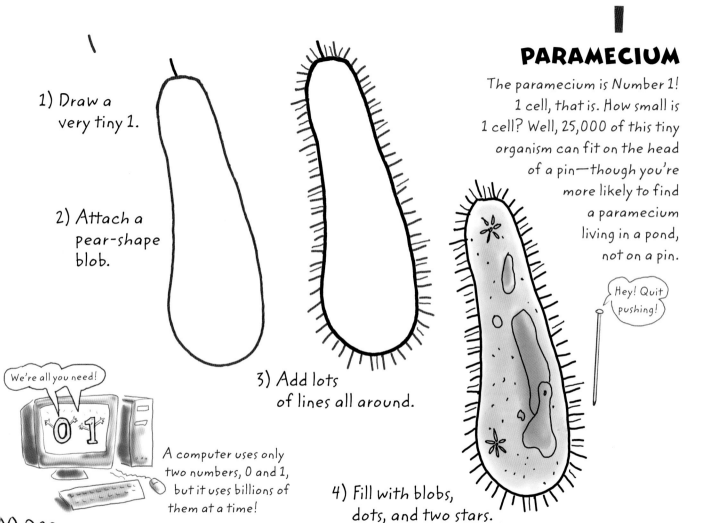

00,000,000,000,000,000,000,000,000,000,000,000,000,000,000,000,000,000,000,000,000,000,000,000,000,000,000,00

2 TOUCAN

You, too, can draw a toucan!

1) Start with a 2.

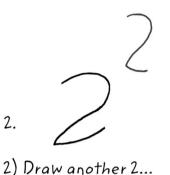

2) Draw another 2...

3) connect the 2's with a curve and attach curvy lines to make a beak.

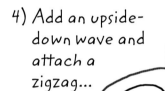

4) Add an upside-down wave and attach a zigzag...

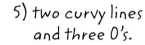

5) two curvy lines and three 0's.

2...4...6...8....
Isn't it odd how almost all animals have an even number of legs?

1) Write 3.

2) Add three more 3's...

3) and a zigzag.

4) Make a big squiggly 6.

5) Add two big squiggles and four little squiggles.

6) Draw two dots and three 0's.

7) Now make a tree for your sloth to hang from.

3
SLOTH

This sloth needs 3 strong toes on each foot since it spends most of its time hanging upside down.

It's a 3-ring circus!

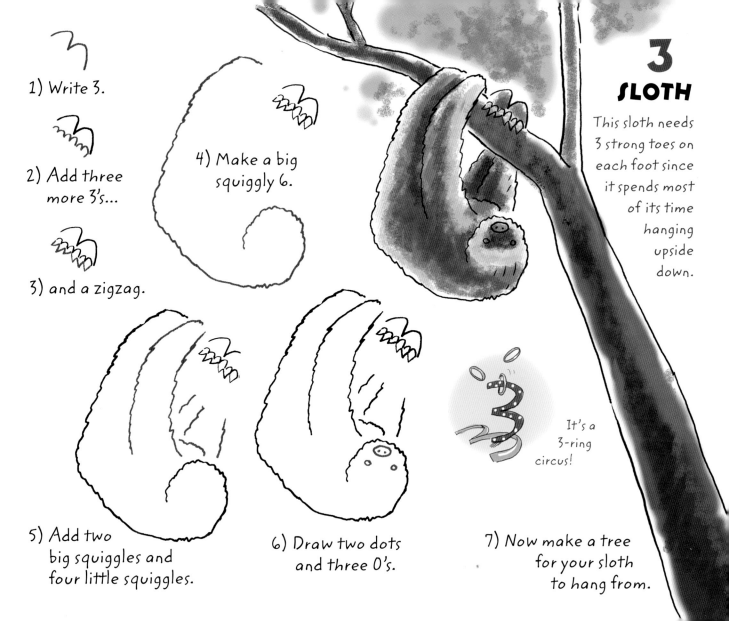

4
HERON

The Great Blue Heron stands tall at 4 feet and spreads its wings to 7 feet.

1) Draw a 4.

2) Put a W on top...

3) and a 9 with a V at the end.

4) Draw a big teardrop around...

5) attach two curvy lines to make a neck...

6) a loopy beak, a 6 eye...

7) and a fish for dinner.

Look at this 4-wheel drive!

Which way did he go? North, south, east, or west?

A pentagon is a shape with 5 sides. The Pentagon is a 5-sided building in Washington, D.C.

What if you had 5 arms like a starfish? You would need two and a half pairs of mittens!

1) Draw a leaning 5.

2) Attach four loopy fingers...

3) two S curves...

4) lines and dots to make a polka-dotted sleeve.

5) Do it all again and then give yourself a hand!

Now that's what I call a high five!

5
HAND

It's easy to count your 5 fingers, but there are a lot of other numbers in your hand! You have 29 bones, 34 muscles, 48 nerves, and 29 joints in each hand.

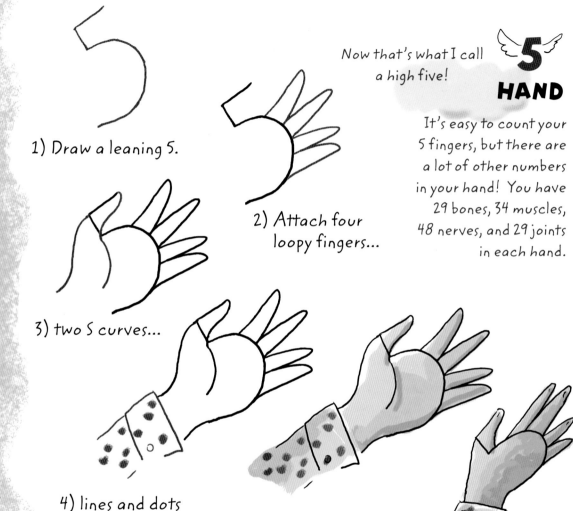

6
RAM

The biggest horns of a Bighorn sheep were 50 inches long.

1) Draw a 6...

2) and another 6.

3) Add a big curve to make the body.

4) Add more curvy lines...

5) a question mark...

6) seven sideways waves...

7) four wedge hooves...

8) and a bunch of woolly blue 3's!

Snowflakes are all different except on one point— they all have 6 points!

1) Draw a big 7.
(The bigger the 7, the bigger your present will be.)

2) Add 3's to make a bow.

Why was 6 afraid of 7?
Because 7 ate 9.

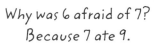

PRESENT

There are 7 days in a week, 365 days in a year, and only 1 day for your birthday present!

3) Draw two right angles to make a square front.

5) Add ribbon and paper—but don't open until your birthday!

4) Connect the front to the back with lines and draw a blue 7.

Look up tonight! Can you find the 7 stars of the Big Dipper?

8
TARANTULA

Tarantulas not only have 8 legs—they've got 8 eyes, too!

1) Draw an 8.

2) Put a small sideways 8 on top.

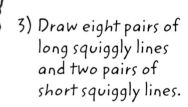

3) Draw eight pairs of long squiggly lines and two pairs of short squiggly lines.

Here is an 8 ball.

Here are some oddballs.

Henry the 8th was an English king who had 6 wives. (But not all at once!)

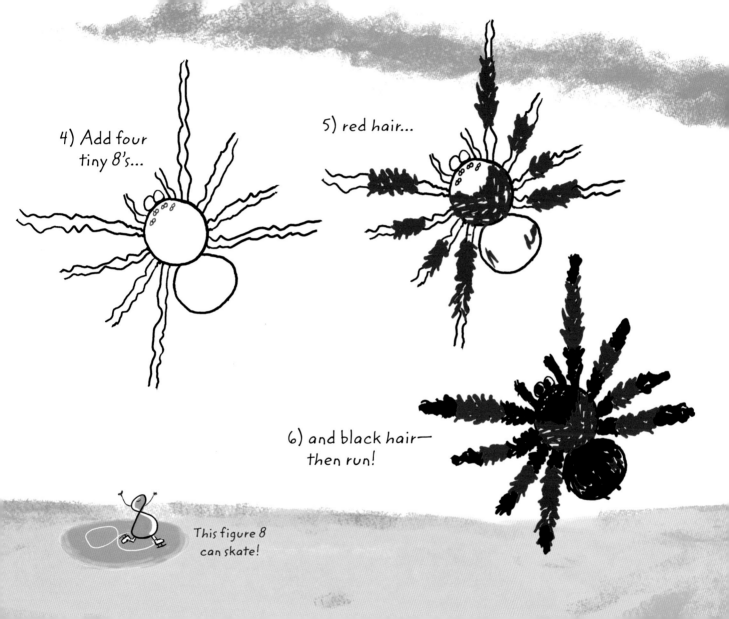

4) Add four tiny 8's...

5) red hair...

6) and black hair— then run!

This figure 8 can skate!

ARMADILLO

9

Check out the 9 planets that orbit the sun in our solar system!

The Nine-Banded Armadillo wears its favorite number around its middle!

1) Draw a 9.

2) Connect top and bottom with a curve.

3) Add two small curves...

4) two teardrops...

5) and a big C.

6) Attach nine curves...

7) then one big curve.

8) Draw three funny-looking 3's.

9) Add two more 3's...

This cat definitely has 9 lives!

10) a curvy tail...

11) and armor!

10 ROCKET

Start the countdown!
10...9...8...7...6...5...
4...3...2...1...
BLAST OFF!

1) Draw a 10.

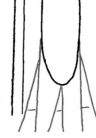

2) Add a long line.

3) Attach four A's.

4) Add two lines to make a right angle.

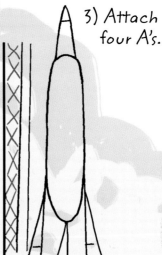

5) Draw ten X's.

Score a strike with a magic 10 triangle.

10 bowling pins are set up in a triangle with 1 in the 1st row, 2 in the 2nd row, 3 in the 3rd row, and 4 in the 4th row.

Scoring 10 on the Richter scale can be dangerous. That's the top for earthquakes!

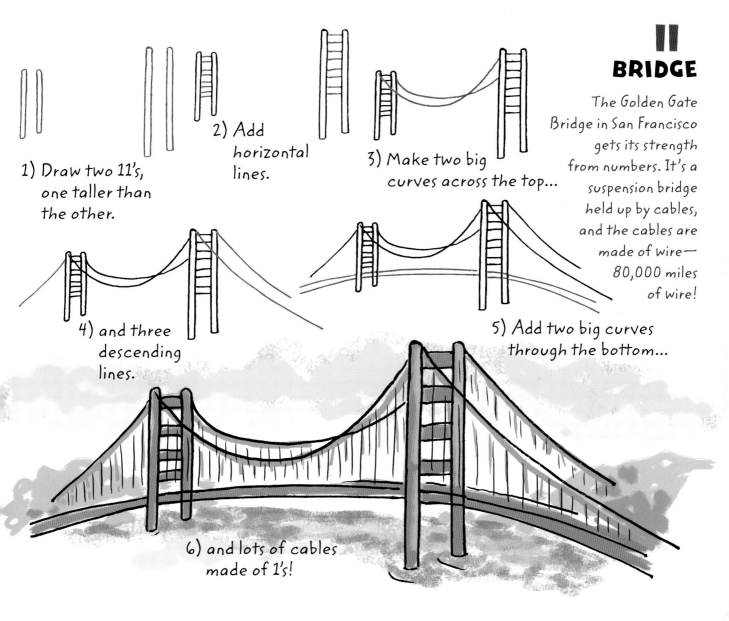

1) Draw two 11's, one taller than the other.

2) Add horizontal lines.

3) Make two big curves across the top...

BRIDGE

The Golden Gate Bridge in San Francisco gets its strength from numbers. It's a suspension bridge held up by cables, and the cables are made of wire— 80,000 miles of wire!

4) and three descending lines.

5) Add two big curves through the bottom...

6) and lots of cables made of 1's!

12
GUITAR

Most guitars
have 6 strings.
12-string guitars
have 6 pairs
of strings.

When does a dozen
equal more than 12?

When it's a baker's dozen—
1 extra is added by
the baker for 13 treats.
That's yummy math!

1) Draw a 12.

2) Add a 3...

3) and two
lines, one
straight and
one curvy.

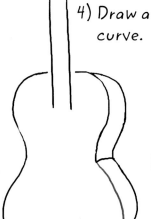

4) Draw a
curve.

5) Add a wedge,
a 0, and a
rectangle.

6) Draw two
vertical
rectangles
and 12 dots.

7) Now string
your guitar
and strum!

1) Draw a 13...

2) and another 13.

3) Add a small d and b for eyes.

Why are there 13 stripes on the American flag?

13 CAT
The unlucky black cat has 13 unlucky ribs.

4) Add four curved lines with little 3's next to them.

5) Draw another curve and two 3's...

6) and make the cat's arched back of little 1's and 3's.

7) Add another curve and more 3's...

8) and color your unlucky cat.

For the 13 original colonies.

CRANE

Numbers have pull!
Cranes use pulleys
to pull more weight
with less effort.
How much less?
A single pulley can
lift a 100-pound
weight with only
50 pounds
of force.

1) Draw a 14.

2) Make boxes of
each number.

3) Add an angle...

4) and two slanted
rectangles.

5) Add a line
and an arc.

6) Draw another arc
and a squashed 0.

7) Now draw another arc
and another squashed 0.

8) Attach three parallel lines...

9) and another set of three parallel lines.

10) Draw four small curves.

11) Put a 6 on a string and draw three 2's.

12) Add an operator.

15
SNOWMAN

The biggest snowman in the world was made in 1999 in Maine. This giant Frosty was over 113 feet high, had six tires for his mouth, and two tires for his eyes—but they couldn't find a carrot big enough for his nose. His arms were made of two 10-foot trees.

1) Write 15.

2) Add a vertical line.

3) Add a trapezoid with fringe.

4) Add a 2...

5) and a 71.

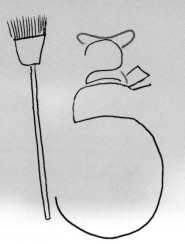

6) Draw a loopy curve and a short line.

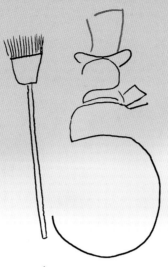

7) Add a 17 on top...

Stack 'em up!
Make 15 snowballs
and put them in a triangle
starting with 5 on the bottom,
then 4, 3, 2, and 1. You've made
a mathematical magic triangle.

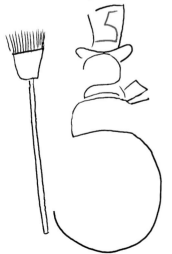

8) with a 5 inside to make a hat.

9) Draw five 0's and fringe.

10) Give your snowman a carrot and sticks.

16
LEMUR

Lemurs live only 1 place on earth—on an island off the coast of Africa called Madagascar.

1) Draw 16 going in two directions.

2) Put a 6 on top.

3) Add curvy lines.

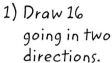

4) Make a little teardrop nose...

5) and add two 10's for eyes.

6) Add lines to make an arm with fingers.

7) Draw scribble stripes to make a ring-tailed lemur.

Who are you calling a square?

Who are you calling a root?

When you multiply one number by itself you get a square number.

$4 \times 4 = 16$ 4 is the square root of 16. Can you think of other square numbers and their roots?

1) Draw a very tall 17.

2) Add another very tall 17...

3) and then a 1 on the left and 7 on the right.

4) Connect all of the ends...

17
SKYSCRAPER

How would you like a job washing windows at the Sears Tower in Chicago? There are only 16,000 windows on 110 floors.

5) and make 16,000 windows!

With numbers you can always count higher!

18
TRUCK

Big trucks need big numbers to haul big loads! Many have 18 wheels, 10 gears, a 140-gallon fuel tank, and an engine 10 times the size of your family's car. That's so they can carry 8,000-pound loads.

1) Draw 18 sideways.

2) Now do it again.

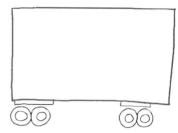

3) Connect them with a big rectangle.

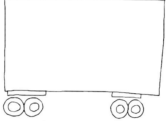

4) Add 47...

5) and connect with lines.

6) Draw a double 0 and perpendicular double lines to make an exhaust pipe.

7) Then hop in the driver's seat and start trucking!

1) Write 19 very slowly.

2) Attach a curvy line...

3) and big spiral to make a shell.

4) Add three small curves...

5) then two vertical lines.

6) Make two dot eyes...

7) and a trail of snail slime.

19
SNAIL

How slow does a snail go? That depends on the snail, of course. Some speedsters zoom along at 55 yards per hour—but slowpokes plod along at 23 inches per hour!

20
DRUMMER

Drummers count!
1-2-3-4. 1 and 2 and 3 and 4!
Keep the beat with math!
It takes a lot of steps
to draw this drummer,
but you 'll march along
when you take one
step at a time!

1) Draw a 20.

2) Put a 0 around
the first 0.

3) Attach an angle
to the 2.

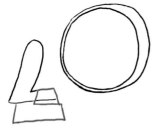

4) Add two wedges...

5) and lines.

6) Draw loopy hand...

7) and a line with a
little 0 on top.

I've got 20-20!
That means I can see
what a normal person
can see at 20 feet.

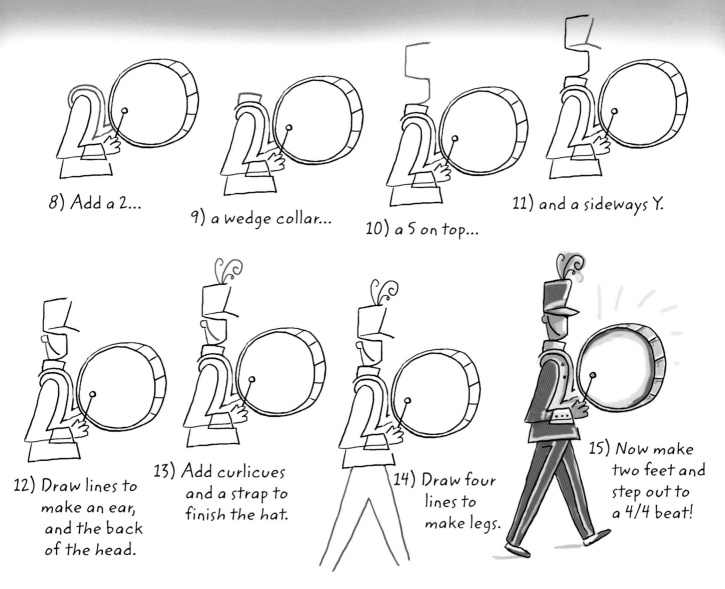

8) Add a 2...

9) a wedge collar...

10) a 5 on top...

11) and a sideways Y.

12) Draw lines to make an ear, and the back of the head.

13) Add curlicues and a strap to finish the hat.

14) Draw four lines to make legs.

15) Now make two feet and step out to a 4/4 beat!

I add up!

$6 + 5 + 4 + 3 + 2 + 1 = 21$

SWANS

You're not seeing double!
Almost all swans mate
for life, so you'll usually
see 2 at once.

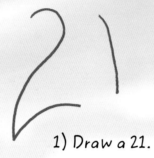

1) Draw a 21.

2) Attach a curve
to the 2.

3) Add two tiny 9's...

4) two tiny 6's...

5) and two tiny 7's.

6) Draw two 2's
with curvy bottoms.

7) Add six weird 3's.

8) Draw curvy lines to make wings for the first swan...

9) and curvy lines to complete the other swan.

10) Now make 21 ripples.

22
DRAGON

Are you a dragon? In the Chinese horoscope you are one of 12 animals, depending on the year you were born. You're a dragon if you were born in 1940, 1952, 1964, 1976, 1988, or 2000. Can you see the pattern in these numbers? Hint: think about how many animals there are in the horoscope. What year will the next dragons be born?

1) Write 22.

2) Attach a sideways 9.

3) Add 770.

4) Put a sideways 3 on top...

5) and a sideways 63 below.

6) Add two loops.

7) Attach an S curve.

8) Add six 2's...

9) and four little 0's.

Now that's what's called standing on your own 2 feet!

And that's what's called dancing in a 2,2!

10) Make a tail from two big 2's.

11) Add angles to make the feet.

12) Attach squiggle wings and ziggy claws.

13) Finish with lots of green 2's and four red curlicues.

23
WHALE

Talk about big babies!
Blue whales can be 23 feet long
at birth and grow to
103 feet long, making them
the biggest animals
in the world!

1) Draw 23 with the 2
far away from the
stretched-out 3.

2) Attach them with
a long curve on top...

3) and a long curve
on the bottom.

4) Add a big teardrop
and a little 9 eye.

5) Now spout
four blue
curlicues!

24 KING

4 and 20 blackbirds
baked in a pie.
When the pie was opened,
the birds began to sing.
Wasn't that a dainty dish
to set before the king?

1) Draw 24.

2) Add 48...

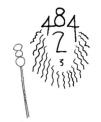

3) a 3 and lots
of squiggles.

4) Put three
circles on top
of a stick.

24 hours
a day. That's
how long it
takes the
Earth to spin
around once.

5) Draw a 6 and
two curlicues.

6) Draw two
more curlicues.

7) Add four curves.

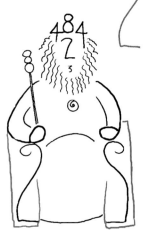

8) Then four lines
on each side.

9) Add two curved lines at
the top to make a throne.

1) Write 25.

2) Add curves and specks...

3) three 6's...

KUDU

The horns on this antelope are longer than its legs—one of the biggest pair ever found measured 61 inches. Imagine running around with your legs on your head!

4) two teardrop ears and two more curves.

5) Attach a big bean-shape body.

I'm 25!

Why is a quarter worth 25¢?

25 is one-fourth of 100 cents. One quarter is the same as one-fourth.

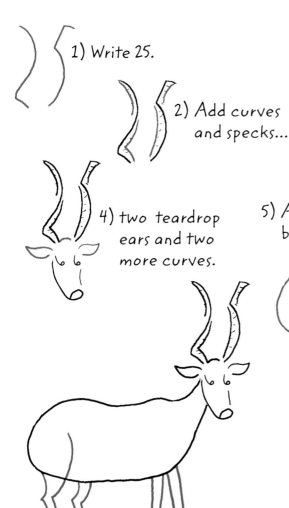

6) Add four sideways waves and four straight lines for legs...

7) four wedge hooves and fringe tail and beard.

26
BRACHIOSAURUS

One of the largest dinosaurs, this herbivore had 26 teeth on its top jaw and 26 teeth on its bottom jaw. Since it weighed as much as 16,000 pounds, it did a lot of chewing.

1) Draw a 26 with a very big 6 and a tiny 2.

2) Connect the numbers with a little point.

3) Add a long curve.

4) Draw two loopy curves.

5) Attach curved lines to make legs.

6) Add ziggy toes.

7) Attach a pointy tail.

This tree is 50 feet tall!

27
MAD HATTER

Lewis Carroll, who wrote about the Mad Hatter in *Alice in Wonderland*, was a mathematician. He made up this riddle: Which clock works better, one that loses a minute a day or one that doesn't run at all?

1) Write 27.

2) Connect the numbers with a 2.

3) Make a square in the middle and wedges around it to make a bow.

4) Add a v and a 7 to make arms.

5) Draw a curve...

6) and put two angled lines on top.

The one that doesn't run—
because it's right twice a day.
The other one is never right.

7) Add squiggle hands and...

8) two small curves and a 0 mouth.

9) Draw two Y's with tails...

10) and a W with feet.

11) Draw two curves and an upside-down V.

12) Put 10/6 on the hat. (Read the story to find out why!)

28
CAMEL

One hump or two? Arabian camels have one hump and can travel 100 miles a day across the Arabian desert. Their hairier, two-humped cousins, the Bactrian camels, live in colder climates and carry big loads—400 pounds and more.

1) Draw a 28.

2) Add curvy lines and a 10 to make a face.

3) Draw a squiggly curve in front...

4) and curves to finish the body.

5) Attach curvy and straight lines to make four legs.

6) Finish with four curvy feet and a fringe tail.

Me!

So, who's perfect? Here's why: Take all the factors of 28 (other than 28 itself)

1 × 28 = 28
2 × 14 = 28
4 × 7 = 28

Add them together:
1 + 2 + 4 + 7 + 14 = 28
They equal 28! Perfect!

1) Draw 29.

2) Add another 29.

3) Add some feathers.

4) Draw two curves.

5) Add curvy and straight lines to make two legs.

6) Add more lines to make feet.

29
OSTRICH

It's the big bird! The largest bird in the world is 7 feet tall. Don't challenge the ostrich to a foot race. Ostriches can run 40 mph—but since they weigh over 300 pounds, they can't get off the ground.

What number appears only once every four years?

Is it leap year yet?

30
SLAM DUNK

Score 2 points when you put the basketball in the net from this close. Score 3 points if you shoot the ball from 22 feet away.

1) Draw a 30...

2) and another 30.

3) Add five horizontal curves...

4) and five vertical curves.

5) Attach two long curved lines...

6) and a wave.

7) Add an S with a hairy top.

8) Draw lines to make a shirt and gym shorts.

31
CLOCK TOWER

Try wearing Big Ben on your wrist! Before people made clocks small enough to wear, they used to make them big enough for everyone to see—and hear. Big Ben's 13-ton bell chimes the time in London, England.

Speaking of time, this number rings out the old year!

DECEMBER
31

1) Write 31.

2) Write 31 again.

3) Put a line on top.

4) Draw a wedge...

5) with a 4 on top.

6) Add four short lines...

7) three long lines...

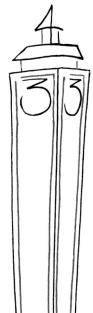

8) and two tall 17's.

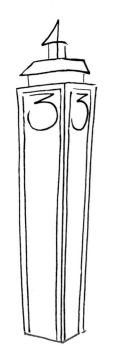

9) Connect the bottom ends.

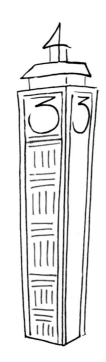

10) Make a pattern of horizontal and vertical lines.

11) Repeat the pattern.

12) What time is it?

32
CHAMELEON

This three-horned chameleon likes to keep its altitude up. It lives in trees in the high mountains of East Africa.

1) Draw 32.

2) Attach 37.

3) Add 50 and a slice...

4) a swoopy 6...

5) and connect with a bumpy curve.

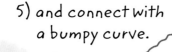

BRRRRR! I'm freezing!

32 degrees Farenheit is the freezing point—when water turns to ice.

6) Add three toes and make your chameleon turn green.

1) Draw 33.

2) Attach an arch.

3) Add four loopy legs and toes.

4) Add 976...

5) and a long, sticky 3.

Toads and frogs are really old— they first appeared 200,000,000 years ago!

3 3 TOAD

People spend 33% of their lives fast asleep.

Say this quickly three times: Three trees of thirty-three threes!

34
TAP DANCER

Tap dancers count with their feet! They shuffle, step, and stomp to make the beat—a 1 and a 2 and a 3 and a 4!

1) Draw a vertical 34.

2) Put on two 13 shoes.

3) Add a line...

4) two zigzags...

5) a hat...

6) two arms...

7) and two loopy hands.

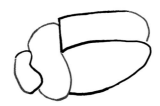

1) Write 35.

2) Connect with curves.

3) Make lines to form antennae.

4) Draw two 6's, one backwards.

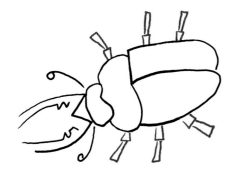

5) Make leg segments with boxes and lines.

35
BEETLE

There are 370,000 different kinds of beetles.

The smallest is 1/32 of an inch or about the size of this speck :

The largest is 7 inches, which is a little longer than this page: →

6) Add 12 squiggle lines to make six creepy crawly feet.

36
MOOSE

This isn't Bambi! Moose are BIG! They can weigh up to 1,800 pounds, with antlers up to 6 1/2 feet wide.

1) Draw a 36.

2) Add wavy lines.

3) Make an S curve.

4) Make a curvy line with fringe.

5) Draw a big squiggly body.

6) Add straight and curvy lines to make legs.

7) Make a green lake.

My yard is bigger than that!

A yardstick measures 36 inches.

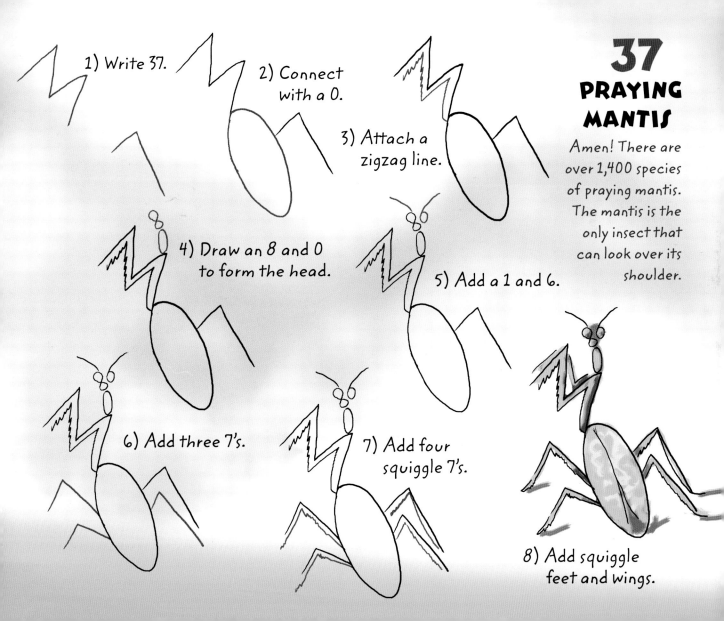

1) Write 37.

2) Connect with a 0.

3) Attach a zigzag line.

4) Draw an 8 and 0 to form the head.

5) Add a 1 and 6.

6) Add three 7's.

7) Add four squiggle 7's.

8) Add squiggle feet and wings.

37
PRAYING MANTIS

Amen! There are over 1,400 species of praying mantis. The mantis is the only insect that can look over its shoulder.

38
SNAKE

Here's a creature with backbones— over 120 of them! That's the number of vertebrae in many snakes, though there are some whose spines are made up of as many as 585 bones.

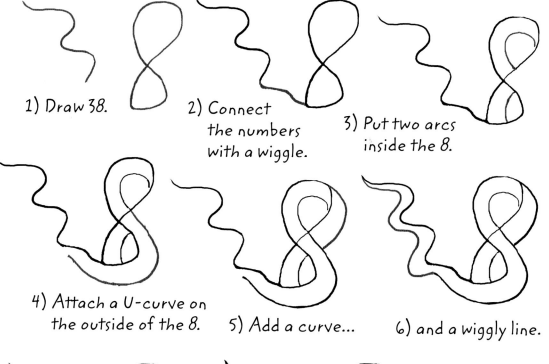

1) Draw 38.

2) Connect the numbers with a wiggle.

3) Put two arcs inside the 8.

4) Attach a U-curve on the outside of the 8.

5) Add a curve...

6) and a wiggly line.

7) Draw a curvy head.

8) Add an eye and a tongue.

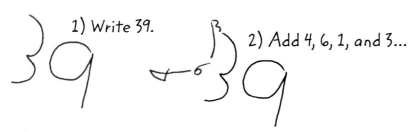

1) Write 39.

2) Add 4, 6, 1, and 3...

3) two slices...

4) and two perpendicular lines.

5) Add two sideways waves...

6) a big slice tail...

7) a big curve on top, two little curves on bottom...

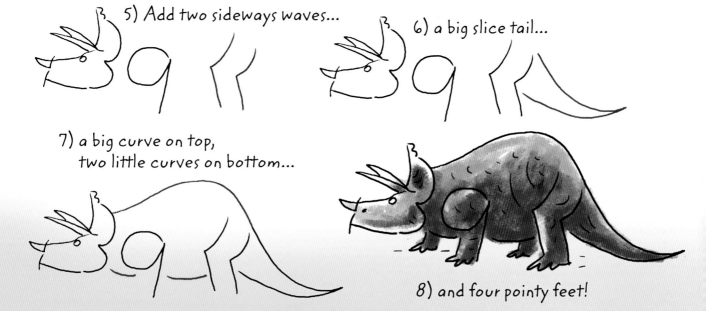

8) and four pointy feet!

39
TRICERATOPS

This really is a dinosaur of threes! Its name means "three-horned face." It was about 30 feet long, of which 1/3 was its big head, and the two horns over its eyes were 3 feet long.

40
LOCOMOTIVE

Locomotives can weigh as much as 440,000 pounds. No wonder they need to let off steam!

1) Write 40.

2) Add two rectangles with curved ends.

3) Attach a headlight...

4) 971...

5) two 0's...

6) and two big rectangles.

Clickety-clack, clickety-clack, Engine No. 40 is steaming down the track!

7) Add two double lines...

8) and two more rectangles...

9) three smokestacks...

10) a bell and an engineer!

41

CASTLE

Castles were built with thick walls for protection. Try knocking down a wall that's 20 feet thick!

1) Write 41 three times.

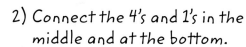

2) Connect the 4's and 1's in the middle and at the bottom.

3) Add three right angles.

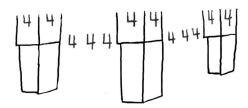

4) Add twelve small 4's.

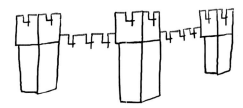

5) Connect at the top...

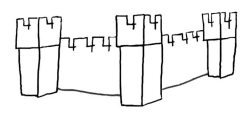

6) and the bottom.

7) Attach 141 at the top.

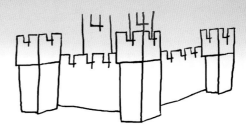

8) Now do it again.

9) Connect at the top.

10) Draw seventeen small arches
for windows and one arched doorway.

11) Add three pointy flags
and dig a moat!

42
PUFFIN

Puffins can fly—in the air and underwater. They can reach 55 mph airborne if they really work at it by beating their wings up to 400 times per minute.

1) Write 42.

2) Attach a curvy 3...

3) and add a 9 eye.

4) Make a big curve on top...

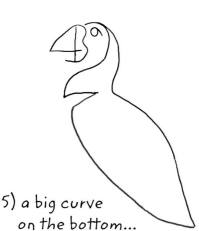

5) a big curve on the bottom...

6) and a big curve in front.

7) Give your puffin curvy orange feet.

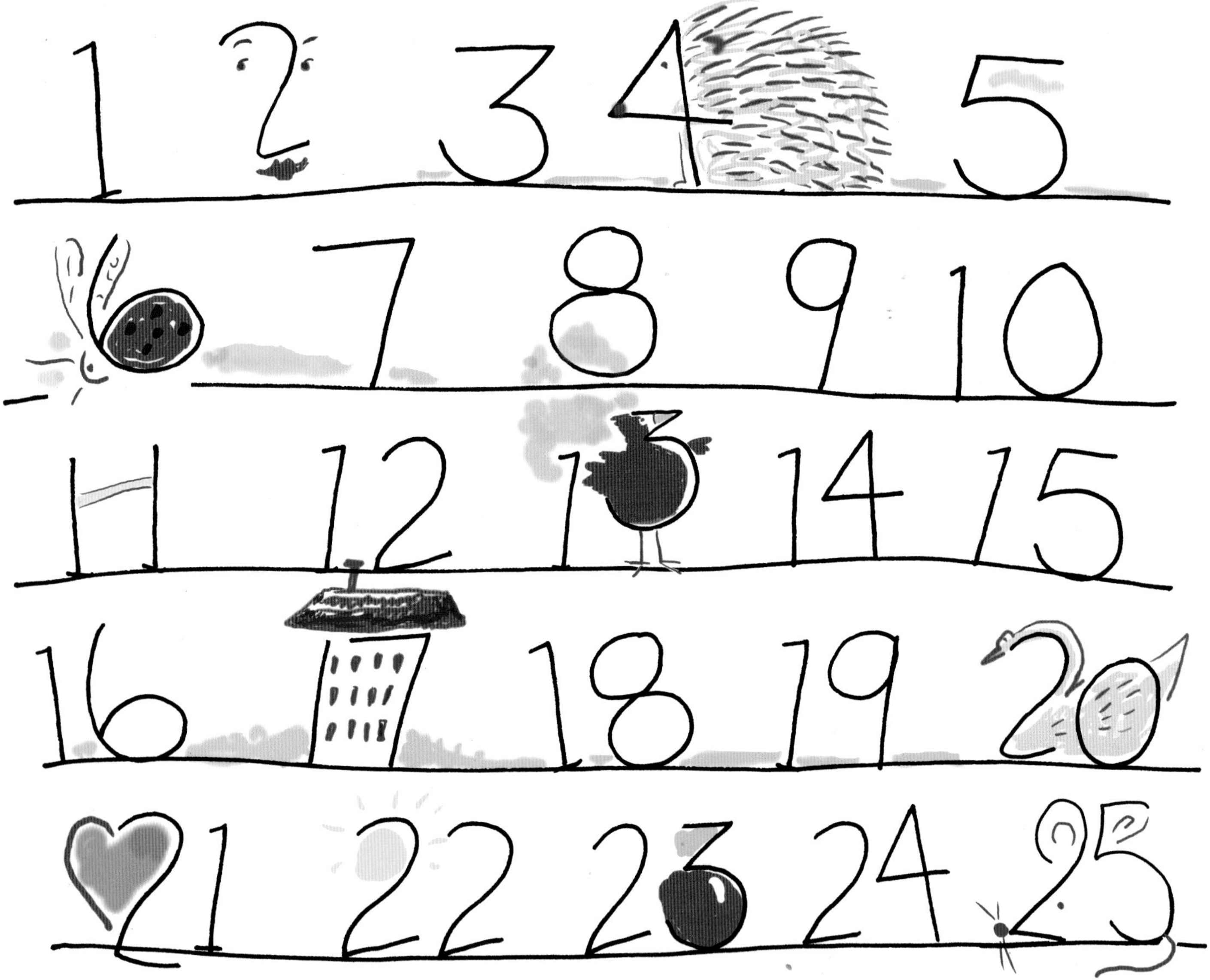
1 2 3 4 5
6 7 8 9 10
11 12 13 14 15
16 17 18 19 20
21 22 23 24 25